Between Heaven and Earth

HOWARD NORMAN

Between Heaven

and Earth

BIRD TALES FROM AROUND THE WORLD

Illustrated by LEO & DIANE DILLON

GULLIVER BOOKS
HARCOURT, INC.

Orlando • Austin • New York • San Diego • Toronto • London

To Emma
To Jackson
To Alexandra Altman
— H. N.

For Anne, Liz, and Ivan
—L. & D. D.

Library of Congress Cataloging-in-Publication Data
Norman, Howard A.
Between heaven and earth: bird tales from around the world/Howard Norman;
illustrated by Leo & Diane Dillon.
p.   cm.
"Gulliver Books"
Summary: A collection of folktales from around the world, all of which have
a bird as a main character.
1. Tales.   2. Birds—Folklore.   [1. Birds—Folklore.   2. Folklore.]
I. Dillon, Leo, ill.   II. Dillon, Diane, ill.   III. Title.
PZ8.1.N77Di   2004
398.24'528—dc21   2003007874
ISBN 0-15-201982-0

First edition
A C E G H F D B

Manufactured in China

The illustrations in this book were done in
colored pencil and watercolor on Bristol board.
The display type was set in Truesdell Italic.
The text type was set in Truesdell.
Color separations by Bright Arts Ltd., Hong Kong
Manufactured by South China Printing Company, Ltd., China
This book was printed on totally chlorine-free Stora Enso Matte paper.
Production supervision by Sandra Grebenar and Ginger Boyer
Designed by Ivan Holmes and Leo & Diane Dillon

Contents

Introduction ◆ vii

The Disobedient Pelican Daughter   AUSTRALIA   ◆   1

The Troll and the Scarf Made of Crows   NORWAY   ◆   15

The Beautiful Quail   SRI LANKA   ◆   31

The Bird Who Sang Like a Warthog   MATABELELAND   ◆   45

The Swan-Scholar's Great Secret   CHINA   ◆   61

About the Stories:
LAUGHTER, ARGUMENT, FRIENDSHIP   ◆   75

Introduction

For centuries in folktales throughout the world, birds have been featured in myriad roles. Birds make their familiar and surprising presence known, and are quite capable of complicating the lives of human beings in unpredictable ways. In folktales birds can be magical, smart, stupid, drab, colorful, wily, obnoxious, elusive, selfish, shy, bold, hauntingly silent or as magnificently loud as a storm, equally capable of enchantment and treachery, but they are always interesting.

The five stories presented in these pages are from Australia; Norway; Sri Lanka; Matebeleland, in Africa; and China. I first heard them in the International Folklore Workshop held at the University of Maryland in 1989 and 1990. I describe that workshop at the end of this collection.

In thinking about the emotional and literary dimensions of these stories, two quotations served as constant companions. The first is from Tabuboku Shinoda, a thirteenth-century Japanese artist who lived in a small house by the sea and who specialized in ink drawings of birds. He wrote:

I have been drawing shore birds. Each evening when they fly off to their secret haunts for the night, I am not merely a little forlorn. The cries of the birds I have drawn echo in my heart, as though my heart were the beach itself. So, to keep the birds a close presence through the dark hours, I repeat to myself stories I heard as a child, stories from the old days, when birds seemed to praise people more knowledgeably, and people comprehended the lives of birds more gracefully, all within the inexhaustible language that is Nature.

It is impressive how the bird stories of Tabuboku Shinoda's childhood continued to sustain him in old age.

The second quotation from which I drew inspiration comes from the great seventeenth-century Chinese traveler Hsu Hsia-k'o, who wrote:

To watch birds fly out over a mountain lake is to have the world itself widen in time and space, to allow the heart and mind to accompany the magnificent flight, to experience the winged creatures' lifting joy between Heaven and Earth.

My hope is that the stories in *Between Heaven and Earth* offer readers a sense of elation about these winged creatures and a chance for their imaginations to soar.

HOWARD NORMAN
East Calais, Vermont

The Disobedient Pelican Daughter

L ong, long ago, when the Noongahburrah people in this corner of Australia went fishing, first they would build a wall of strong grass and creeper across the creek. Then the people stepped into the creek a ways upstream from the wall. Starting there, they kicked and slapped along—and sometimes they sang a fish-catching song:

> "In the harsh sun
> and wind so strong
> it is as if everything might be swept away,
> and the world would have to start over—
> we step into the coolness

of the creek,
slap the water, slap the water—
fish, fish, fish, fish, fish—
a feast tonight, a feast tonight!"

—driving the fish against the wall. At the wall, they easily caught the fish and tossed them onto the banks.

At other times, when the rains had fallen for days in a row and the creeks were in flood, the Noongahburrah people would build a smaller wall along a tributary creek. When the rains stopped and the creek shrunk to puddles, the people would simply pick up the fish that had been left behind, flopping in small puddles, scuttling about in the shallowest of shallows, poor fish, with not enough room for both the fish and their shadows.

It took a long time to build such walls, but knowledge of how to make a fishing net had not yet been given to the Noongahburrah people. Net making was still a secret known only to Goolayyahlee, the pelican.

Now, being a pelican, Goolayyahlee of course could hold many fish in the pouch of skin at his lower beak. Sometimes his children would reach in with their bills and nab a fish or two for themselves.

Goolayyahlee was the best fisherman in the territory. The crocodiles were good fishermen. The kingfishers were good fishermen. But Goolayyahlee was so skillful that his fishing was considered a kind of magic. And like any good magician, he had a number of secret tricks. For instance, it was said that Goolayyahlee could actually cause it to rain by spitting a fish hard into a cloud. But Goolayyahlee's most closely held secret by far was where he hid the one and only fishing net in all of Australia.

When Goolayyahlee and his pelican children were about to go fishing, he would say, "Now, fly off and get eurah sticks for the end of the net!" The eurah was a small, droopy tree covered in big yellow-white bellflowers. It grew near water. Goolayyahlee knew where every stand of eurah trees was to be found. Pelicans could gather eurah sticks up and carry them in their skin-basket mouths without hurtfully poking themselves.

"A net, a net, a net, a net!" The Noongahburrah people would hear Goolayyahlee say the word net to his children. They knew the word, but they had never seen a net.

When the little pelicans returned and set the sticks at their father's feet, they saw that the net had already been laid out on the ground. Beside the net, Goolayyahlee would already have started a small twig-fire. Then, Goolayyahlee threw eurah leaves into the flames. "Now, children," he would say, "stretch out the net over the fire in the smoke." Why did Goolayyahlee ask his children to do this? Because the eurah tree was

3

sacred, and its sticks and leaves provided good luck, so when the net was held in the smoke, it assured that the fishing would be a great success. The little pelicans were allowed, then, to place the eurah sticks they had gathered into the fire. But always some sticks were saved to start the next fire.

And the net truly made fishing easy. Two pelicans held it while the others—including the youngest—chased fish down the creek. A pelican's shadow racing along the surface of the water is a frightful thing to a fleeing fish. Finally, all the pelicans dove into the net, gulped down many fish, and flung the net onto land, where Goolayyahlee waited for his share.

"There is one fish left!" a pelican child would shout.

Now, Goolayyahlee could make a spectacular show of spinning and whirling through the air, scooping up the last fish. Instead, he always said, "Let it go! Let the last fish go, so that more fish might be here tomorrow."

Once they had feasted on fish, the pelicans would fold their legs, hunker down, and sleep in the wind and sun.

One day, the most mischievous and inquisitive and disobedient of the pelican daughters decided to try to discover where the fishing net was kept. In the past, when this disobedient daughter had said, "Father, where do you keep the net?" Goolayyahlee

warned her, "That is my secret. Do not try to find out." Many times Goolayyahlee had warned her. Still, this daughter wanted to find the whereabouts of the net, and nothing could stop her! She waited until Goolayyahlee was asleep in the wind and sun, and then set out on a journey.

This pelican daughter knew that when Goolayyahlee woke up, he would count his children. When he saw that she, the disobedient one, was missing, he would get storming angry. The truth was, Goolayyahlee's anger could actually cause storms! Lightning. Thunder. This was the magic talent that the disobedient daughter most loved, admired, and enjoyed—when her father got mad, a spectacular storm would sweep in.

The disobedient daughter flew high in the air and low to the ground. The sun was merciless. The winds were whistling in her ears. She flew along. She flew along. And as she flew, she sang:

> "To the net, to the net,
>   to the net where it hides,
>   my father will be angry I went
>   to the net where it hides."

Oh, she was happy flying along, out to locate the secret hiding place of the net.

She passed through a region of parched red earth, where thousands of cracks webbed out in the shape of an enormous net. She passed through a region of trees, whose branches were shaped like woven nets waving in the air. She flew on for days. And each time she looked down, she saw the shape of a fishing net! "Am I awake, or am I dreaming all of this?" she said.

On and on she flew. She could not remember, now, if she had flown in a straight line, in circles, or had merely weaved this way and that, utterly lost. Finally, she stopped.

She sat near some boulders. "I must sleep," she said. She closed her eyes. But right away, she heard a sound unlike any she had ever in her life heard. She peeked out from behind a boulder, and there she saw her father, Goolayyahlee!

Goolayyahlee was doing very strange things. He stretched his neck, waggled his head, stood on tiptoe, hiccupped, undulated his throat, burped, gulped many times in a row, stretched out his neck, rattled his pouch, clacked his bill, and hopped high into the air. When he landed, he made a loud choking sound, as if a fishbone were caught in his throat; opened his mouth wide—and out flew the fishing net! It floated beautifully in the air a short distance, drifted to the ground, and spread to its full width.

The disobedient pelican daughter was amazed. Here, she had traveled for days through territories full of strange net shapes, flown under scorching sun, fighting winds so strong it was as if everything would be swept away and the world would have to start over again—wind, sun, wind, sun—and here, she had ended up at her father, Goolayyahlee. The secret of the net was in her own father's stomach! "I have traveled far from home," she said, "and yet I am also back at home."

She then leapt out into clear view. "Father!" she cried. "I saw you roll the fishing net out of your throat! I saw this!"

"I warned you not to go looking for the net!" Goolayyahlee said.

To guarantee that her father would get truly storming angry, the disobedient pelican daughter said, "Yes, you did. And what's more, Father, I heard you warn me clearly."

Goolayyahlee got storming angry.

The storm that Goolayyahlee's anger set loose was entirely made of lightning. First, he made the sky black. Then he zigzagged lightning along the horizon. The lightning webbed across the black sky.

"I know you are angry, Father," the pelican daughter said, "but this lightning does you proud. You would not have made such a beautiful and powerful lightning storm had I not angered you in such a manner. You are a great magician. This storm has pleased your daughter greatly."

Goolayyahlee fluttered his wings wildly, squawked, clacked his beak, but made no attempt to punish his daughter. He was defeated by her intelligent flattery. "Very well, then," he said. "The secret of the fishing net has been discovered and there is nothing I can do about it. Let us return home."

Goolayyahlee and his daughter flew home side by side, pulling the net in clear view behind them.

When they finally landed near their home creek, all of Goolayyahlee's other children gathered around.

Goolayyahlee held up the net. "My clever, disobedient daughter traveled a long ways," he said, "and discovered where I hid the fishing net. I swallow it. The net has always been kept inside my stomach. But, truth be told, I am tired of swallowing it day after day, year after year. I have decided to show all of my children—and all of the Noongahburrah people—how to make a fishing net!"

Goolayyahlee then sent his children out to gather together the Noongahburrah people. "Tell them to meet us here by the creek," he said. The pelican children scattered in all directions.

Once the Noongahburrah people had arrived, Goolayyahlee said, "Now, I am going to tell you how to make a fishing net. First, you strip the bark off a noongah tree, take off the hard outside, and then chew the inside until it's soft enough to be made into a sort of string. It is from that you make your net—you just knot the string up into squares.

"Now, since I am a magician, all I had to do was swallow the soft part of the bark and the string, and then the net just made itself inside my stomach.

"But you people must practice weaving a net. You will get it wrong many, many times. But someday, the weaving will turn out just right. Then you will have the perfect fishing net! That is a promise."

That night, the first feast ever held between the Noongahburrah people and the

pelicans took place. They shared a big meal of fish. The Noongahburrah people cooked their fish, but the pelicans simply gulped theirs down. After the feast, they all sat by the fire. The pelican daughters told many stories about how they angered Goolayyahlee, and how they were entertained by Goolayyahlee's storms. Then the Noongahburrah daughters told their own stories about angering the Noongahburrah fathers. There was much laughter, and just for fun, Goolayyahlee caused a spectacular storm on the horizon. At dawn, the Noongahburrah people left the pelican's creek, setting out to find eurah trees and begin their new life as net weavers. They were grateful to Goolayyahlee for this important knowledge.

Some say it took the Noongahburrah people a whole generation to get the net woven in such a way that no fish could escape. But knowledge could last forever.

To this day, pelicans can still make nets inside their stomachs. Goolayyahlee taught them that magic. The name *Goolayyahlee* means, "He who has a net."

The Troll and the Scarf Made of Crows

The fjord crows favored Old Olav Sverdrup's wind-off-the-sea yard more than any other yard in Olav's village. The crows were always loud. Olav had to feed them ten loaves of bread every evening to quiet them down, or else he simply couldn't sleep.

This particular night, it was important for Olav to get a good night's sleep. He had to be up early the next morning to sharpen his granddaughter's ice skates. Her name was Elise. She was ten years old. Tomorrow was the ice-skating race along the winding creek that led from the sawmill to the fjord and the sea.

So, Olav baked ten loaves of bread and tossed piece after piece to the gathered crows, until finally they were satisfied, bellies full, and stopped *caw-cawing* for bread. The crows settled down for the night.

As a child of ten, Olav himself had won a prize on skates. The prize he had won was for performing the most curlicues as the judge counted to sixty. Even now, though he was an old man, Olav's heart beat wildly when he thought back to his victory. The whole village had watched! But the very next day, when he had entered the ice-skating race, disaster struck. He and the other children had lined up across the width of the frozen creek, all poised and bent in anticipation, anxious for the starter to clap his hands. The starter clapped his hands, and between the clap and the echo, the children were off! They raced side by side at first, then, of course, as in all races, some children skated faster than others. Soon, Olav got into the lead. He was far out front. The inland wind was pushing at his back and he could already taste the salt-sea air in his mouth as he got closer to the fjord and the sea—and then the wind off the sea took over from the inland wind, and the skating was much more difficult. But still, Olav kept well ahead of the other children.

Olav was going at a steady pace, when suddenly, out from a small cave along the creek, leapt a troll with a scarf made of live crows! The wings of the crows were folded over one another as tightly as the scales of a black fish, and the crows were all at once *caw-caw*ing loudly. The sound was deafening. The troll kept perfect balance on the ice and quickly caught up with Olav, and when the troll got right alongside, he unraveled his scarf. The crows beat their wings against Olav, and Olav could scarcely believe what

was happening. Finally, Olav careened off the ice and fell facedown into the snow.

When Olav lifted his face from the snow, he heard the other skaters race by, on to the fjord and the sea. Later, when the judge of the contest, the starter, and all the villagers asked Olav, "What happened?"—and Olav's own mother and father asked, "What happened?"—Olav told the truth. Everyone said they had heard that exactly such a troll wearing exactly such a scarf lived in a cave along the creek. And they were all sorry this troll had leapt out at Olav. "But, still," said the judge, "you've come in last place."

Olav grew up, married, and his wife gave birth to a daughter; her name was Nan. But sadly, Olav's wife died from a spill off a cliff, right where the inland wind met up with the wind off the sea, and so Olav was left to raise Nan alone.

At just three years old, Nan was already a splendid ice-skater. She fairly flew over the ice. Every winter morning, Olav sharpened his daughter's skates. Nan was just six years old when she entered her first big village race, which began at the sawmill and ended at the fjord and the sea.

The evening before the race, the crows in Olav's yard were very loud and annoy-ing, so Olav baked ten loaves of bread and tossed piece after piece to the crows until they hushed down, huddled together, and slept. Olav got a good night's sleep, woke early, and sharpened his daughter Nan's skates, then walked with her to the sawmill.

Everyone in the village was there. Soon, the race began. Right from the start, Nan flew off ahead of all the other children. Olav was proud. But when Nan got near the small cave, out leapt the troll! The troll loosed his crows at Nan, who lost her balance and careened into the snow. As the other children raced by, Nan shouted, "Watch out for the troll! Watch out for the crows!" But the children paid Nan no heed, because the troll and his crows were nowhere in sight!

Though she loved her father very much, when Nan got married, she and her husband left the village. "When I have a child," she said, tears in her eyes, "I will come back here to live. That is a promise."

Time passed and Olav waited patiently for his daughter, Nan, to return. One day, there was a knock on his door. When Olav opened the door, there stood a ten-year-old girl. "I am your granddaughter, Elise," the girl said. Standing out in the yard kicking at crows was Olav's daughter, Nan, and her husband. They had a happy reunion with Olav. "We are now living in a house in the village, here," Nan said. "Just the other side of the sawmill."

That brings us up to the present time in our story.

Now, let it be known that knobby-headed, squat trolls with broom-bristle hair and voices as if they are chewing on stones were quite familiar to the people of the village. Everyone saw a troll now and then. Once in a while, a troll would steal a church pew to use for firewood. Once in a while, a troll family would be seen leading a muzzled white bear along a far ridge. The bear's fur was so thickly matted that only the strong wind off the sea could preen it, which was why trolls took the white bear to the top of the ridge. To the villagers far in the distance, it was like seeing small people out for a stroll with a cloud. Once in a while, a troll would cause serious mischief of one sort or another in the village. But by and large, the villagers had lived in peace for centuries with trolls in the vicinity. Oh yes, there was that one time when trolls raided a henhouse and left only a few eggs and feathers. And yes, there was that time when trolls snuck into the village and took baths in the butter churns. But by and large, villagers and trolls got along quite well. Trolls might bring good luck or bad luck—different folk believed different things. A troll might steal a church pew, but the villagers figured they could always carve a new pew, and who could really blame trolls for wanting to stay warm by a fire?

Olav himself was not peevish about trolls. He was not at all frightened by them. He was not superstitious about them, either. He merely considered trolls part of village life. He was an old man. He had seen trolls since he was a child. He never once had run cursing and waving a stick at a troll. Yet he had never invited a troll in for soup or tea, either. Truth be told, Olav never harbored much of a grudge against the troll who had ruined his chance to win the ice-skating race, and who had ruined his daughter's chance

to win. He was wary of that troll, but he did not spend a moment's time hating him. In fact, a scarf made of crows seemed to Olav to be an admirable invention, really—after all, if you live in a stone cave, you have to keep warm.

Still, with the big skating race coming up, Olav was quite worried about his granddaughter. He could not bear the thought of her getting ambushed by the troll and his crows. Yet he did not want to warn Elise of the troll. He knew knowledge of the troll might worry Elise and make her timid about that turn in the creek where the troll's cave was located, and maybe she would be a little afraid.

So, Olav woke very early. He sharpened his granddaughter's skates. Sparks flew from the grinding wheel. He prepared a pot of hot broth and waited for his granddaughter to come into his house without knocking, as only she was allowed to do. The ice skates were on the splintery table, the very same table Olav had eaten at as a child, the same table he had eaten breakfast, lunch, and dinner at his whole life. And soon Olav's granddaughter walked in. "Good morning, Grandfather," she said. "Are my skates ready?"

"As you see," said Olav.

Olav set a bowl of broth next to the ice skates.

"Grandfather," said Elise, "would you like me to comb out your beard? Your beard is quite unkempt and I've brought a comb."

"No," said Olav. "Just sit down and sip some broth."

"Would you like me to comb your hair for you, Grandfather?" asked Elise. "It is as ruffled as a crow's feathers in the wind."

"No," said Olav. "Just sit down and sip some broth. It's cold out and you'll need strength for the race."

"Grandfather," said Elise, "let me pluck a hair from your head and test the sharpness of the blades."

"Very well," said Olav.

Elise plucked a hair from Olav's head. She stretched the hair tautly, then ran it over an ice-skate blade—the hair was cut fast in two. Elise looked tremendously happy.

She took three sips of broth. "I don't mean to boast," she said, "but I think I may have a chance to win today's race. I've raced the other children before and beaten them soundly, and if I keep my wits about me, I might do well, don't you think, Grandfather?"

"I think it's best not to boast before an accomplishment, nor boast after," Olav said. "But kept as a secret between you and me, yes, I believe you will do yourself quite proud, my dear granddaughter. Now, have a few more sips of broth."

After Elise took a few more sips of broth, she stood up from the table and said, "Let's not be late!"

It was lightly snowing. Old Olav walked with his granddaughter, skates slung over her shoulder, to the sawmill. The entire village was gathered there. Elise put on her skates, then laced them tightly, with an extra piece of twine snugly around each ankle. She got lined up across the width of the creek with the other children. She bent over slightly. She whispered, "The fjord and the sea, the fjord and the sea," over and over, but so only she could hear. The starter clapped his hands, and between the clap and its echo, off went the racers! Soon, they made the first bend and were out of eyes' view.

After all of his years in the village, Olav knew every shortcut to the fjord and the sea. He had herded sheep along the shortcuts. He had walked weeping along the shortcuts, mourning the death of his beloved wife. He had taken shortcuts that were loud and boisterous with crows; he had taken shortcuts that were so quiet they seemed bandaged in fog. He had taken a shortcut to the fjord and the sea, and taken the long path back to his house. He had taken the long path to the fjord and the sea but then taken a shortcut home.

He knew a shortcut to right where the troll's cave was. So, the moment his granddaughter rounded the first bend, Olav set out as fast as his old legs would carry him. He was walking on snowshoes. The snow began to fall harder. Also, he had to keep shifting shoulder to shoulder the sack he carried, which was packed with loaves of bread.

After a while, he got to the top of the snowy rise, and when he looked down into the valley, he saw his granddaughter, Elise, skating swiftly along the frozen creek. She

was a sight to behold! Tears of joy replaced tears caused by the stinging wind. Olav had never seen such a joyous sight—his beloved granddaughter was a hundred broom-lengths ahead of the child in second place.

However, Olav's granddaughter was also getting nearer and nearer to the troll's cave, so Olav had to hurry. He knew the troll was capable of hearing the scratching of ice skates far in the distance, no matter how loud the wind. He knew the troll most likely was already hunched at the cave mouth, instructing his crows what to do.

Leaning into the harsh wind, Olav snowshoed up behind the troll's cave. Standing off to one side of the cave mouth, Olav blew into his cupped hands, trying to warm them. He then reached into his sack, took out a loaf of bread, and broke it into small pieces, tossing each piece in front of the cave but not out onto the frozen creek. He did not want his granddaughter stumbling over a crow! Because the wind was just so, in the distance Olav heard his granddaughter singing, "The fjord and the sea, the fjord and the sea, the fjord and the sea! . . . " And coming from inside the cave, Olav heard, "Caw! Caw! Caw! Caw!"

Olav now scattered all the rest of the bread, except for one special loaf, out over the snow. He called out, "Caw! Caw! Caw! Caw!"

Finally, the troll stuck his head out of the cave and grumbled, "What's this? What's this?"

The troll was of course wearing his scarf made of crows, and when the crows saw all of the bread out on the snow, they unraveled and flew from the troll's neck and swooped down for a feast!

The troll was furious—he hopped about and snarled at the crows, "Have I not fed you daily? Have I not allowed you to stay warm in my cave? Why do you forsake me in so bold a manner?"

Now, Olav had studied the crows in his yard, and he knew that crows indeed have good memories, unlike other birds that seem to have weak memories or no memories at all. So, the troll was smart to try to appeal to the crows' memories. But crows always remember to take whatever is offered them at the moment. Bread! Olav was delighted that the entire scarf of crows was now scattered on the snow, bickering and squalling over crusts of bread, the bread Olav had baked precisely for the purpose of distracting the crows away from his ice-skating granddaughter.

However, all was not yet safely fixed in Elise's favor—not quite yet. Because, as she rounded the curve and sped toward the section of creek so nastily guarded by the troll, the troll shouted, "I'll trip her up myself!"

The troll stood in the middle of the creek, waiting for Olav's granddaughter.

But Olav had suspected something like this might happen. He reached into his sack and took out the last and biggest loaf of bread; it was braided like a horse collar.

Olav had baked it weeks before, let it harden and stale, stiffen like wood. Now, Olav rushed forward and collided with the troll. They both fell backward into the snow. "What's this? What's this?" cried the troll.

Olav had forced the braided loaf of bread over the troll's head. Before the troll could tear it off, the hungry crows descended on their master and pulled so hard at the loaf, trying to tear off a splinter, they lifted the troll right up into the air. They carried the troll out over the fjord and the sea.

Now, Olav's granddaughter rounded the bend and when she saw Olav, he was performing curlicues on his snowshoes in the middle of the creek! "Why, hello, Grandfather!" Elise shouted. She skated right on past.

When Elise reached the final bend before the fjord and the sea, she looked up ahead and saw crows hovering a troll high in the air.

I must tell Grandfather about this flying troll, she thought. *My grandfather will believe that I saw it, of course.*

The Beautiful Quail

On a scorching hot day in the second year of drought, everyone in a poor village in the northwest province of Sri Lanka gathered around the stone well. The old bucket-man, Mr. Goonewardene, lowered the splintery bucket to the very bottom. He then leaned over the well lip and shouted, "We are thirsty!"

The well echoed, *"We are thirsty! We are thirsty! We are thirsty!"*

Then, as if riding the last echo, up flew a beautiful quail. The quail landed on the well lip. "The well is empty," she said.

"No water left at all?" said Mr. Goonewardene.

"I have drunk the last drop," said the quail. "It will scarcely be enough to get me through until I lay my eggs."

"We are wishing you good luck, Quail," said Mr. Goonewardene. "For a world without quails would be a heartbroken world, indeed."

"But what will you do without water?" said the quail.

"We must pack our few meager belongings and set out to find a village that will share its water with us," said Mr. Goonewardene.

"Good-bye, then," said the quail.

"Good-bye, good-bye," said Mr. Goonewardene. "We will miss terribly your soothing voice at dawn and the rustling of your charcoal-tipped feathers at dusk."

"I will miss the smell of your spicy midday soups," said the quail, "and the sound of children laughing under the moon."

The quail watched as the villagers walked away down the dusty road.

Now, the beautiful quail was ready to lay her eggs. But she did not want to build her nest on the sun-cracked ground in the field of brittle weeds. She did not want to nest on the rust-colored clay of the abandoned school yard. She did not want to lay her eggs inside the one iron rice-cooking pot. Nor on the pile of rough burlap millet sacks, which were stacked under the bamboo table in the empty marketplace.

The beautiful quail called out to a group of monkeys, "Bring me the mattress old Mr. Goonewardene sat on day and night. He was bucket-man for sixty years. If the mattress was good enough for him, it is indeed good enough for me!"

The monkeys obeyed, and soon the quail sat on the mattress. "Now," said the quail, "set all sorts of pillows around me."

The monkeys brought twenty pillows of all different shapes, colors, and sizes, and arranged them around the quail.

"Now, my friends," said the quail, "kindly bring me my betel leaf and areca nut, and place them at the corner of my bed, for they will bring me good luck."

Quickly, the monkeys brought a betel leaf and an areca nut and set them in the proper place on the old mattress.

"Now, leave me alone," said the quail. "It is time for me to lay my eggs."

The monkeys scurried off and disappeared inside the village huts and meeting-house and market stalls.

The beautiful quail prayed for rain in her most soothing voice. It was a simple prayer. "Please rain," she said softly. "Please rain. Please rain."

The quail then closely studied the mattress. Old Mr. Goonewardene had long ago embroidered a scene from his childhood on it, a very colorful scene, wherein his mother and father were drinking great gulps of cool water from the village well. And though its yarn had unraveled some and the colors had faded in the sun, anyone could still see that it was a picture of great happiness.

The quail arranged the pillows to her satisfaction. She situated herself directly atop the water well in the embroidered scene. She closed her eyes and daydreamed of the cool water beneath her. It was now dusk. The beautiful quail sang for a while and soon fell asleep.

But in the morning, just at dawn, when she awoke and saw that her eggs had not tumbled forth, the beautiful quail did not sing. Instead, she fell into a deep sadness. Her sadness was as deep as the deepest gullies in the northwest province.

Finally, at noon in the blistering heat, she sang:

"What is the use of sitting and staying?
What is the use of betel leaf and areca nut

at the corner of my bed?
O Philosopher Elephant, please saunter by
in the wavering heat,
misstep and send me to Heaven.
For what is the use of life?"

Just then, trudging out of the forest, Philosopher Elephant stopped directly in front of the quail. "I will not step on you," Philosopher Elephant said. "Instead, I'll stand close and shade you from the merciless sun. For the sun is already merciless even at this early hour. And look, I'll spray you with water I sluiced up from a river that had shrunk to merely a puddle, miles from here."

The elephant lightly sprinkled the quail, and she felt as if she had been touched by a moist silk cloth of ocean breeze.

"Thank you, dear Philosopher Elephant," said the quail. "Your philosophy of shade rather than a philosophy of sorrow is most helpful just now."

And the elephant stood there all day, sometimes with eyes closed, swaying or holding boulder-still in the harsh sun. Then at dusk, heavy eared, heavy shouldered, heavy footed, the elephant moved slowly down the road, each step a small cyclone dust-up choking the air. The beautiful quail saw the dust hanging in the air long after Philosopher Elephant was gone from her sight.

Alas, the beautiful quail slept fitfully that night, and in the morning, when she saw that no eggs had tumbled forth, she once again grew sad. Hers was a deep sadness. As deep as the deepest gullies in the northwest province.

She sang:

> "What is the use of sitting and staying?
> What is the use of betel leaf and areca nut
> at the corner of my bed?
> O Philosopher Jackal,
> you who have always prided yourself
> on being able to scare up
> peacocks, weaverbirds and quail
> from our hiding places,
> please devour me, now—for I am in clear view.
> For, O Philosopher Jackal,
> what is the use of this life?"

A jackal, tongue lolling out and panting and wild eyed, now stumbled dizzily out of the forest. "It is true," said the jackal, "I am half starved and delirious in this heat.

In any other circumstances, I would devour you and then sit on this fine mattress and take a nap. But I won't do so while you try to lay your eggs. For a world without quail would be a world without quail for my very own children to eat, would it not? Instead, I will share with you the last of my wild plums, whose sweet juice will keep you alive. They are precious plums in a time of drought, to be sure."

The jackal set three plums next to the quail. "Good luck, then, in your egg laying," the jackal said.

"Thank you, thank you, Philosopher Jackal," said the quail. "Your philosophy of eating plums rather than a philosophy of sorrow is most helpful just now."

The jackal and the quail each took a bit of plum, sucked hard down to the pit, nibbled a little more plum until their faces were stained with plum juice. Then the jackal trotted ever so slowly down the dusty road.

That night, the beautiful quail hardly slept at all. In the morning, when she saw that no eggs had tumbled forth, she again grew sad. She could only stare longingly at the embroidered water well on the mattress beneath her. Even before dawn, it was scorchingly hot. She had eaten the last plum, and the taste of plum juice was only a memory. She had to somehow try to get through the day. It would be difficult, but she had to try, for the sake of her unborn children. But by noon, as though hypnotized by the heat, the quail saw something that wasn't really there, a mirage: *In the wavering*

heat of the dusty road, there walked side by side Philosopher Elephant and Philosopher Jackal,
and when they got close, they collapsed to the ground and became puddles of water, and the
quail leaned down to drink. . . .

Just then, a loud clacking noise startled the quail back to her senses. The quail
looked up from the mattress. An enormous crocodile, dry mud flaking from her back
and legs, was so heat-crazy that she was snapping her toothy jaws at nothing at all!

The quail sang:

> *"What is the use of sitting and staying?*
> *What is the use of betel leaf and areca nut*
> *at the corner of my bed?*
> *O Philosopher Crocodile,*
> *the news has reached me that your children*
> *shriveled up dead on the dry mud flats.*
> *Come, Philosopher Crocodile,*
> *who is to say that death's darkness*
> *is not like an endless*
> *drink of cool water?*
> *Come close your jaws over me, please,*
> *for what is the use of life?"*

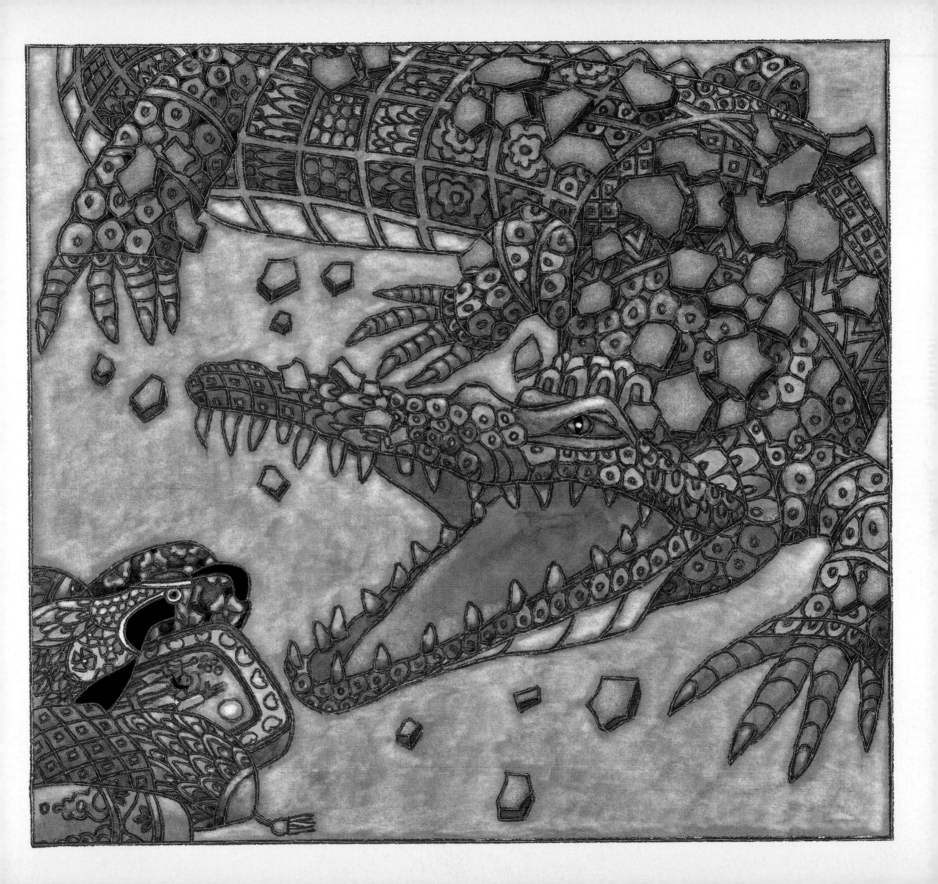

The crocodile lifted up on her four legs, and dragging her thick tail, approached the beautiful quail. "It is true," said the crocodile, "my children have perished in the drought. And it is true that I got so thirsty, I drank seawater, whose salts have made me thirstier yet and caused me, now and then, to snap at the ghosts of my children flying at my eyes. But no, no, I will not close my jaws over you, Quail. And why is that? Because I myself am dying, can you not see this—or does my ancient grin hide all secret expressions from coming forth? For it is little known that crocodiles have opinions and moods as various as the birds in the jungle trees. No matter, no matter. I am dying, and my last desire is to hear you, Quail, sing the soothing song I have heard every day of my life in the river. Everything I loved most happened every day. I shall miss the world so! Please, Quail, sing for me."

And so, the beautiful quail sang. The crocodile listened, and when she was satisfied, she crawled back out to the dry sun-cracked river bottom and died.

"O Philosopher Crocodile, thank you, thank you!" cried the quail. "Your philosophy of soothing music, rather than the philosophy of sorrow, is most helpful just now."

The beautiful quail did not sleep all night. At dawn, she slept, but only for a few moments, because she was awakened by raindrops hitting her face.

It rained and rained. It rained all morning. It rained all afternoon.

At dusk, Philosopher Crocodile tumbled away in the rushing current of the river.

Philosopher Elephant sluiced up water from the river with his trunk. Philosopher Jackal splashed with her children at the river edge.

And then—then—the quail's eggs tumbled forth. The beautiful quail sat on them in the rain.

She closed her eyes and slept.

And when next she awoke, she saw old Mr. Goonewardene next to her, mending the scene of his childhood with darning needle and yarn.

It rained until the eggs hatched, rained while the hatchlings huddled near their mother, rained as the servant monkeys held a tattered umbrella over the beautiful quail, rained at dusk. The beautiful quail was too weary to sing. And so, it is said that the first lullaby heard by the quail children was rain.

The Bird Who Sang Like a Warthog

In a village near the Matopos mountains, lived a young man, Kumalo. He made life irritable for everyone around him by bragging, "I know every animal voice with my eyes closed!" He had bragged this since he was a boy, bragged it all through his young adulthood, and now as a man bragged, "I know every animal voice with my eyes closed." There was little doubt that Kumalo would brag it as an old man, too. It was irritable bragging—but everyone was used to it.

The truth was, Kumalo was fairly skilled at recognizing animal voices with his eyes closed. But he wasn't nearly as good as Sibanda, a blind man his own age. Sibanda had been born blind. And from the time he could first talk, he impressed the elders of the village by how he could recognize the voices of animals, even though the bush must have been for Sibanda a great darkness. Sibanda was especially good—in fact, perfect—

at figuring out bird voices. He never was wrong. And there were many, many, many different kinds of birds in the bush!

"Do you want to brag about it?" the elders would ask Sibanda.

"I don't need praise," Sibanda would say. "True skill at something is its own blessing."

Sibanda had a beautiful younger sister. Her name was Limpopo—she was named after the Limpopo River, because her mother gave birth to her just after crossing the Limpopo River. By and by, Kumalo married Limpopo, and they moved into the same hut. Limpopo looked after her brother, Sibanda, cooked for him, walked alongside him whenever they traveled outside the village, sang to him at night. In return for her kindness, Sibanda sat with Limpopo out in the bush, and Sibanda would guess at animal voices. That Sibanda was so good at guessing animal voices delighted Limpopo no end. No end to her delight. "It is a gift to listen to you guess bird voices," she would say. "But I think my husband is jealous. He tries hard, yes, but he often mistakes one bird for another."

"I've sat guessing animal voices with him," said Sibanda. "He always gets a warthog right."

"Yes," said Limpopo, "a grunting warthog is one animal voice my husband never gets wrong."

But Limpopo was disturbed. She knew her husband well. Her speculation about Kumalo's jealousy worked its way into her everyday thoughts, and she was very worried; it worked its way into her every-night thoughts, and she could not sleep for fear that her husband might do Sibanda harm.

"Kumalo is a good man," Sibanda said to her one day when they were out walking. "He provides for you. He is not greedy. He did not complain when he had to carry heavy calabashes of water in the burning hot sun, that time when beestings swelled your legs and made it impossible for you to walk. He tended you back to health, too. And remember that time he chased off hissing hyenas from the child who wandered out, whose parents were carelessly bickering, facing in the wrong direction? He chased off those hyenas, Kumalo did, with only a rock and a stick."

"He has done good deeds," said Limpopo. "He is my husband. I do not speak badly of him; I only speak truthfully about a bad quality. My husband's jealousy of your skill at recognizing animal voices—especially birds—troubles me deeply, my brother. Be careful when you are alone with him."

"He asked me to go bird trapping with him tomorrow," said Sibanda. "I am pleased to be asked."

"You are stubborn," said Limpopo.

"Is stubbornness a bad quality?" asked Sibanda.

"Not good or bad," said Limpopo. "But if stubbornness allows you to put faith in the wrong person, it could do you harm."

The next morning, Kumalo said to Sibanda, "Let's go into the bush. I want to try to trap a colorful bird."

They set out walking into the bush. Kumalo carried two woven traps. Kumalo walked a few steps ahead. At first, they followed a path that was very familiar to Sibanda—he didn't even need his walking stick to guide him. But after a while, Kumalo led them off into the thicker bush, where thorn trees and other trees grew close together, a place where there were many animals on the ground and birds in the trees. They walked for a long time. All the while, they each guessed at animal sounds.

"There are warthogs nearby," Kumalo said. "Warthogs just a few steps away, behind some trees, at a water hole. Hear them?"

"Grunting and slurping up water," said Sibanda. "Good job, my brother-in-law. Excellent."

"What do you hear?" asked Kumalo.

"I hear the sound of a bird's wings unfolding," said Sibanda, listening intently. "The bird is preening, wing feather by wing feather—one, another, another feather, another—now, the wings are folded back tight to the body."

Kumalo's heart was filling with jealousy, the way a calabash fills when it is held underwater. Jealousy was filling Kumalo's heart quickly. Still, Kumalo's jealousy only revealed itself in words of praise. "Your hearing skills are most impressive," he said.

They walked on, finally reaching a place where Kumalo could set up two traps. "Let's stop here," he said to Sibanda.

"Very well," said Sibanda. "Limpopo tells me you are very skilled at disguising traps with vines, rocks, and leaves in a way that no bird discovers until it is caught."

"That is true," said Kumalo. "I am setting our traps in such a way."

But Kumalo lied. Indeed, he was hiding one trap in a place birds were likely to come for water, disguising it with vines and grasses. The second trap, however, Kumalo did not bother to disguise at all. He just set it out in the open, away from water. Then they went home.

The next morning, as they approached the traps, Sibanda said, "I hear birds in our traps. Definitely, birds are caught."

It was true. Kumalo pushed back the vines, reached into the hidden trap, and pulled out a bird. But it was a drab bird. It was dull and dingy, with little color at all. Then he looked over at the trap that was out in the open. He felt filled with jealousy. The bird in the trap he had intended for Sibanda had in it a bird so magnificent, it was as if it had flown through a rainbow and been stained by the colors. The feathers from such a bird would make a fine present for Limpopo. Kumalo thought he could pluck a few feathers, then keep the bird in a woven cage. This way, Limpopo could wear the feathers and also hear the bird sing.

Kumalo quickly put the drab bird into Sibanda's trap, and put Sibanda's rainbow bird into his own trap. "Yes," he then said to Sibanda, "we have both caught birds."

"Let me touch my bird," said Sibanda.

"Very well," said Kumalo. He held out the trap with the drab bird in it. "The trap is right in front of you—reach out for it."

Sibanda reached into the trap, then ran his fingers over the bird's wings, breast, and tail. Without saying a word, he shut the woven trap and fastened the vine latch.

"Oh, such good fortune," Kumalo said.

"Yes, good fortune," said Sibanda.

Each holding a woven trap—one bird singing, one silent—Sibanda and Kumalo walked home.

On their way home, the two men stopped to rest under a broad-leafed shade tree. As they sat there, they talked about many things. Every now and then, Sibanda said, "Shhhh—listen." They both would fall silent. Then Sibanda would name a bird voice. "Indeed, you have a true skill," said Kumalo, his heart filled to the brim with jealousy.

"Why do you think people fight with each other?" asked Sibanda.

"That is a difficult question," said Kumalo. "Why, brother-in-law, do you suppose that people fight?"

"They fight because they do to each other what you have just done to me," said Sibanda.

Now, since Kumalo's heart was completely filled with jealousy, there was no room for shame. He tried lying again. "I do not know what you mean," said Kumalo.

Hearing this, Sibanda reached out, unfastened the vine lock from his woven cage, and set free the drab bird. The bird flew high up in the leaves of the tree. Then it began to sing, "Liar, liar, liar, liar, liar," in a sweet and beautiful voice.

"Do you recognize that bird voice?" said Sibanda.

"No," said Kumalo. "I have never before heard that voice."

"You will be hearing it quite often," said Sibanda.

They set out again for their home village. Along the way, they heard fluttering in the leaves above their heads. "Shhhhh—listen," said Sibanda.

They both fell silent, then heard, "Liar, liar, liar, liar, liar, liar, liar, liar," in the sweet and beautiful voice.

"Why are we not hearing other birds?" cried Kumalo. "Why are we only hearing this one bird?"

"Even in a bush full of birds, sometimes one voice is heard most clearly," said Sibanda.

"I will let my bird go," said Kumalo. "Its voice will drown out that hideous call."

"Is it a colorful bird?" asked Sibanda.

"As if it had flown through a rainbow and was stained by the colors," said Kumalo.

"Let it go, if it pleases you to do so," said Sibanda. "Then listen for its voice."

Kumalo opened his woven trap, and out flew the rainbow bird. It flew straight along the ground, disappearing behind some scrub trees.

"Shhhh—listen," said Sibanda.

They both fell silent. Then they heard, "*Grrrrr—tttsssunt, brruppp, brruppp,*" a kind of grunting snort.

"Ah, warthogs," said Kumalo, very sure of himself.

"Not warthogs—," said Sibanda, "a rainbow bird."

"That is a warthog!" said Kumalo.

"Go look for yourself, then," said Sibanda.

Kumalo walked a short ways, pushed back some vines and low bush, and saw the rainbow bird. It was sitting atop a warthog. The warthog, caked in mud, was silent. But

the bird was singing, and the sound it made indeed was, "*Grrr—ttttsssunt, hrruppp, hrruppp,*" grunt-snort, grunt-snort, grunt-snort!

Kumalo walked back to where Sibanda stood. "I saw a warthog with my own eyes," said Kumalo.

"And what perched on the warthog?" asked Sibanda. "Because, I heard the sound of a bird hopping along the back of rough warthog skin, lightly scratching, lightly scratching with its feet."

"That was the rainbow bird," said Kumalo. "But it wasn't singing. It wasn't singing at all."

Hearing that song again, Kumalo ran off into the bush. He was full of jealousy, and shame had wedged in, too. Jealousy and shame storming up inside makes a person run faster than ever, as if chased by rhinoceroses or a pack of hyenas. He ran and ran. But Sibanda was not worried at being out in the bush alone. He broke off a low branch and used it as a walking stick. Feeling with the stick along the ground and waving it out in front of him, Sibanda finally found his home village.

"Where is my husband?" asked Limpopo.

"He has run off into the bush," said Sibanda.

"What happened?" asked Limpopo. "Tell me!"

"In my trap was a colorful bird. In his trap was a drab bird. I know its song. Kumalo was filled with jealousy," said Sibanda, telling exactly the truth. "He switched birds—then lied to me about it."

"Oh, my husband—," said Limpopo.

"There's one other thing to tell you," said Sibanda.

"What is that?" asked Limpopo.

"Two birds are driving him out of his mind," said Sibanda. "One is the drab bird, which keeps singing at him, 'Liar, liar, liar, liar.' The other is the colorful bird, which badly humiliated Kumalo."

"Was it the colorful bird that sounds much like a warthog?" asked Limpopo. "The bird that one day, when we were walking together, you recognized as a warthog-sounding bird, not a warthog at all?"

"Yes—that's the bird," said Sibanda.

"Did my husband wrongfully guess it was a warthog?" asked Limpopo.

"Yes," said Sibanda.

"Oh, my poor husband," cried Limpopo. She ran off into the bush.

Limpopo searched in the bush for six days. Finally, she found her husband. He had gone out of his mind. He was sitting in a warthog wallow. His neck, face, shoulders, back, and arms were caked in mud. He was grunt-snorting. The rainbow bird was sitting atop his head. Still, when he saw his wife, he recognized her. "Limpopo," he said, "close your eyes. Listen."

Because she wanted to handle him carefully, Limpopo did what Kumalo asked. She closed her eyes and listened. She heard, "*Grrr—ttttsssssunt, brruppp, brruppp!*"

"What is making such a noise?" mud-caked Kumalo asked.

"A warthog," said Limpopo.

"Wrong—guess again," said Kumalo.

"The rainbow bird," said Limpopo.

"Wrong—guess again," said Kumalo.

"My husband," cried out Limpopo. "It is my husband who made the warthog's grunt-snort!"

Limpopo set up house near the warthog wallow. Each day, she bathed Kumalo with fresh water hauled by calabash, provided meals, and spoke to him late into the night. At first, Kumalo only spoke in warthog grunts. But ever so slowly, he used human language again. Now and then, Limpopo visited her brother, Sibanda, just to see that things were well with him. Finally, Limpopo's caring mended Kumalo back to his senses. It had taken almost a year.

"Are you well enough to return to our village now?" she asked her husband.

"Yes," he said. "I am happy to be going back. My heart is empty of jealousy. Shame, however, may never leave."

"I have news for you," Limpopo said. "My brother is married."

"That is good news," said Kumalo. "Whom did he marry?"

"He married my new sister, Balib," said Limpopo.

"The one who loves to hear the sound of warthogs and who loves to wear beautiful feathers in a necklace?" asked Kumalo.

"Yes," said Limpopo. "She seems very happy with Sibanda."

"Before we return, I must trap a bird," said Kumalo.

Kumalo expertly disguised a woven trap near the stream where he was certain birds would come to drink. He and Limpopo waited overnight. In the morning, Kumalo was happy to find a rainbow bird in his trap. He and Limpopo hurried to their home village.

When Limpopo and Kumalo were invited right away to visit Sibanda and Balib, everyone was happy. Kumalo presented Sibanda's new wife, Balib, with a woven cage. Inside the cage was a bird so magnificent, it was as if it had flown through a rainbow and been stained by the colors.

The bird grunt-snorted in its woven cage. Then, Sibanda reached in and plucked ten feathers from the rainbow bird. He gave them to Balib.

"I have been out of my mind—to be truthful about it," Kumalo said to Sibanda.

"I am glad you no longer are, friend," said Sibanda.

They sat down and had a meal together. It was the first meal Sibanda's new wife, Balib, had prepared for relatives. It went very well. After the meal, Balib braided the feathers into a necklace and put the necklace around her neck. They all sat talking, laughing, talking some more. The bird that looked like it had gotten its magnificent colors from a rainbow sang like a warthog.

The Swan-Scholar's Great Secret

A boy named Chiao lived in the village of P'o-lo at the foot of Dragon Gorge Mountain. His parents were very poor. Every ten days, they walked the treacherous narrow path high along the mountainside to the bamboo forest. There they cut bamboo stalks, tied the stalks up in two bundles, then lugged the bundles on their backs along the return journey to P'o-lo. In P'o-lo, they sold the bamboo to broom and basket makers. They earned a pittance, but Chiao never went without food or clothing. Chiao loved the sound of bamboo stalks clacking in the evening fog, because it meant that his parents had returned. He would run to the edge of the village, and when his parents stepped out of the fog, Chiao would say, "I heard you and now you are here. Set down your bundles. I love you without end."

On the days that his parents were away cutting bamboo, the family's trusted old friend, Li, looked after Chiao. Li was even poorer than Chiao's family and ate every meal at their house. When Chiao's parents were in P'o-lo, Li would take long, solitary walks. One day on just such a walk, Li happened upon a hut. Looking inside, Li discovered that the hut was empty of all human presence except for a piece of embroidered cloth in a dirt corner. On closer inspection, Li saw that it was dark blue cloth embroidered with white swans in various configurations of flight, also preening, squabbling, and elegantly drifting on the water. The blue was the color of sky and water.

"Ah," Li thought aloud, "perhaps this piece of cloth was left here years ago by Hsiang, the famous meandering swan-scholar, the one sent all over China to gather knowledge of swans, to fill his bland pages with drawings of swans, to return now and then to the capital and report directly to the emperor in lively language the temperaments and mysteries of swans."

Indeed, on his last visit, Hsiang had stayed in this very hut, only coming into P'o-lo once or twice to buy turnips. On that visit, Hsiang had remained in the region for thirty days. Each day he had attempted to climb down Dragon Gorge Mountain to Wild Bird Lake. Hsiang had heard a rumor that the swans living at Wild Bird Lake were actually the ancestors of the villagers of P'o-lo, transformed into swans after they had died. Hsiang had been warned against the gorge, told that it was frequented by sudden powerful roars of wind called dragon gusts. A traveler might be ambushed by a dragon gust and plummeted into the gorge. But Hsiang was stubborn and thirty times tried to climb down to Wild Bird Lake. Thirty times he was forced by dragon gusts to turn back. Never in all of his many years' wanderings, in all of his attempts to gaze upon and study swans close-up in the most remote and hidden lakes, had Hsiang failed. When he finally said good-bye to the villagers of P'o-lo, it was impossible for them not to notice how sad Hsiang looked.

Now, Li bent down to pick up the cloth. Touching the cloth, she felt an object inside. She unfolded the cloth, and much to her astonishment, there was a telescope. She had seen a telescope only once; Hsiang, the emperor's swan-scholar, had owned one. Li picked up the telescope. It had two sections that slid out of a larger third section, then locked into place. Li stepped from the hut, held the telescope to her eye, and looked toward Dragon Gorge Mountain. She saw wild swans wheeling high above Wild Bird Lake, but of course could not see the lake itself. Then, setting her sights a bit lower, she peered at her home village, P'o-lo. She saw many villagers going about their daily tasks. Li then folded up the telescope, covered it with the cloth, and set out for P'o-lo.

Li went directly to Chiao's family's house. She handed the cloth bundle to Chiao, who was age ten, and said, "A gift for you, my friend."

Chiao was curious and delighted. He set the bundle on the one table in the house. Chiao unfolded the cloth. He stared at the telescope. "What is it?" he asked.

"A telescope," Chiao's father said. "I have seen only one telescope before. The swan-scholar Hsiang owned one. But his last visit was twenty years ago. Here, let me show you how it is assembled."

Chiao's father locked the sections out at their full length. "There's a full moon tonight," he said. "We can look through this gift at the moon."

That very night, Chiao, his mother and father, and their friend Li took turns looking through the telescope at the moon. They did not talk or eat or sleep. They looked at the moon, both with and without the telescope, the new and old way.

Early the next morning, Chiao's father said, "Your mother and I have to work today in the bamboo forest. Let's pack some food, Chiao. You may accompany us to the highest point of the mountain path. There we will share a meal, take out the telescope, and look at Wild Bird Lake."

Chiao could not have been more excited.

After half a morning's walk, they reached the highest point of the mountain path. Sitting with backs pressed against the mountain, they happily ate their meal and spoke of their sleepless night with the moon. Then Chiao said, "May we look at Wild Bird Lake now?"

"Yes," said Chiao's mother.

Chiao folded out the telescope. He looked through it, adjusting his sight downward. Chiao suddenly gasped with astonished pleasure. "I see it!" he exclaimed. He saw that the shiny lake had not one leaf or twig floating on it. Then he saw a twig fall from a gnarled gorge-tree onto the water, but right away a beautiful swan swooped down and plucked the twig from the lake and set it on land. The swan then disappeared behind a stand of gorge trees. Chiao felt a strangely joyful sensation, as if a ghost had brushed past his face, or a honey-filled raindrop had hit his tongue exactly the way he had dreamed it would. His heart beat wildly.

"What did you see?" asked his father.

Chiao told him about the twig and the swan.

"Yes," Chiao's father said, "if a leaf or twig falls onto Wild Bird Lake, a swan takes immediate notice. Swan-ancestors cannot bear a cluttered lake."

"Why is that?" asked Chiao.

"It is a mystery," said Chiao's mother. "But a mystery that does not diminish your life because you cannot solve it."

"Look again," said Chiao's father. "What else can you see?"

Chiao looked through the telescope. "I see swans in great numbers," Chiao said. "Also, I see ducks and geese. Are ducks and geese also ancestors of our villagers?"

"No," said Chiao's mother. "We have only swan-ancestors."

"Let your mother look now," said Chiao's father.

Chiao handed the telescope to his mother. She looked through it. Smiling, then laughing, she said, "I see my grandparents, aunts, uncles, cousins, and many neighbors who lived in P'o-lo long before you were born, our son. I recognize them individually. It is truly mysterious, how I can tell one ancestor from another, seeing as they are now swans, but it is mysterious in a useful and satisfying way, so who am I to question such a gift of perception from the deities?"

Then Chiao's father looked through the telescope. He, too, recognized aunts, uncles, neighbors, grandparents. Chiao's parents laughed and gossiped about people whom they remembered with great fondness. They gossiped and laughed, gossiped and cried.

To Chiao, it was a delightful education, all of this gossip. Finally, though, Chiao's father said, "We must now continue on to the bamboo. We trust you will be careful walking home. If a dragon gust roars up, flatten yourself to the path, hold on for dear life—remember, you are a strong young man, not a twig plucked up by a swan. Goodbye then, our son. We love you without end."

Chiao returned to P'o-lo and his parents set out toward the bamboo forest.

Just before dusk, Chiao stood at the edge of his village and folded the telescope out to its full length. He wanted to see his parents on the return path. He held the telescope to his eye. It did not take long to find his parents. They were just at the place where, that morning, they had sat, laughing about the moon, gossiping. Chiao's father was a few steps behind Chiao's mother. It was a clear day. Then, suddenly, Chiao's father reached back, tore his bundle from his back, and flung it into the gorge—Chiao's mother threw her bundle into the gorge at nearly the same moment. They both flattened to the path. Chiao's father held on to the feet of Chiao's mother. Chiao knew what he was witnessing: Dragon gusts were ambushing his parents! In the long practiced way of people who carried bamboo on the treacherous path, his parents had done all they could do—they flattened to the path. Chiao's heart beat wildly, as if every swan at

Wild Bird Lake were in his chest, trying to lift off from the water. But in a time too brief even to fit in a prayer of safekeeping to the deities, Chiao's parents were tumbling through the air.

Chiao felt helpless. Why wouldn't his wildly beating swan-wing heart lift him from the Kingdom of Earth to rescue his parents? No, he was only a young man, his feet on the ground, watching with astonished fear as his parents plummeted downward, following the bundles of bamboo stalks. Wild Bird Lake awaited.

Then, clearly though the telescope, Chiao saw his mother and father each turn into a swan. They curved upward, held to a circling pattern a short time, nuzzled, then glided downward, disappearing from Chiao's sight. Even though Chiao could hardly have imagined seeing such a transformation, these words all but flew from his mouth: *"That was beautiful."* Yet, suddenly orphaned, Chiao was deeply shaken. Running toward his house, he wept with confusion, grief, and helplessness. He already knew that the sight of his parents changing into swans would never leave his memory.

Li was setting bowls of rice on the table when Chiao burst in, shouting, "My parents are now swans!" They sat at the table together. Chiao told Li all he had seen. The rice grew cold. No matter. "Tell it again, slowly," said Li. Chiao told everything, slowly. They sat at the table all night and wept and did not sleep. There was a full moon in the sky, but neither Li nor Chiao greeted it. The telescope remained closed up in the blue cloth.

A year of mourning passed in the village of P'o-lo. Chiao had taken up his parents' occupation of bamboo cutter, and showed remarkable skill at it. Each time Chiao set out for the bamboo forest, the basket and broom makers said, "Please, give our regards to your parents." They knew that Chiao always stopped at the highest point along the path to look through the telescope at the swans of Wild Bird Lake. He watched the swans flying, preening, squabbling, elegantly drifting, snaking their heads underwater. When they called out in raspy voices, Chiao was convinced that the swan-ancestors were gossiping. To Chiao, it was equally mysterious and satisfying that he could recognize his mother and father among the many swans. And Chiao always thought, *Who am I to question such a gift of perception from the deities?*

Ten more years went by. Li used a walking stick now. One day, on his return journey from the bamboo forest, Chiao saw up ahead an old, white-bearded man sitting cross-legged, back pressed against the mountain. Chiao sat down next to the old man. "You must be Chiao," the old man said. "In the village of P'o-lo, I was told that you observe the swans of Wild Bird Lake through a telescope."

Chiao folded out his telescope to its full length. "Yes," Chiao said, "it is no secret. And to whom am I speaking?"

"I am Hsiang," the old man said. "I am the emperor's swan-scholar."

Hsiang took out some food from a bundle of blue cloth embroidered with white swans in various positions of preening, flying, squabbling, elegantly drifting. "Would you share a meal with me?" Hsiang asked.

"Gladly," Chiao said. "But first, I suspect that this telescope is the one you left behind on your last visit."

"I left it in a hut at the outskirts of your village," said Hsiang. "It was careless of me. I am fortunate it was handled with such care in my absence. Thank you. Please— keep it. It is now yours." Hsiang took out another telescope, very much like the one Chiao now owned for good. "As you can see, I have another. I have seen many swans through it. But I have never seen the swan-ancestors of Wild Bird Lake."

"Do you actually believe they are my village ancestors?" asked Chiao.

"Yes," said Hsiang. "I do believe that."

They sat cross-legged, backs pressed against the mountain. They were not bothered by dragon gusts. The day was clear. They heard a few dragon gusts in the distance. They were not alarmed. They sat happily talking. They became great friends. Hsiang looked through his telescope. His heart beat wildly when he saw the swans of Wild Bird Lake for the first time. He was deeply pleased. Hsiang and Chiao sat a long time, sharing knowledge of swans. They gossiped. Hsiang said, "I promised never to reveal the secret of the swan-ancestors."

"Not even to the emperor?" asked Chiao.

"A secret dearly held between two swan-scholars will do no harm to the emperor," Hsiang said.

Hsiang stayed in P'o-lo for thirty days. Then, one clear, cold morning, carrying a bundle of food prepared by Li, Hsiang set out on his lifelong wanderings again. Chiao set out in the opposite direction, toward the bamboo forest. He stopped at the highest point of the mountain path. He folded out his telescope. He looked across past P'o-lo and saw his friend Hsiang walking. "Safe, good travels, my friend," Chiao said. He looked down into the gorge, setting his sights on Wild Bird Lake. He found his parents. They were flying over gorge trees, then landed on the water.

Chiao said, "I love you without end," as was his custom.

About the Stories:

The five folktales in *Between Heaven and Earth* were told, discussed with raucous dedication, and eventually edited during twenty-two meetings of the International Folklore Workshop, held in 1989 and 1990 at the University of Maryland in College Park. None of the participants, from eleven countries, took part for academic credit; I had simply advertised the workshop, and they signed up. During each of our four- to five-hour meetings, I learned of their frustration at being cut off from native languages; their profound sense of cultural disenfranchisement; how they remained sad if stoical in the face of unremitting homesickness. Some had held important positions as journalists, teachers, and scholars at home, but political circumstances had exiled them to the United States. Now they were working with great dignity to support families (at home and here) as chauffeurs, gardeners, housepainters, substitute teachers, tutors, bicycle messengers, and so forth.

After the initial few meetings, during which stories were told (first in the language of origin, then in English) and discussed but not recorded, we established two things: First, we intended to create a book. Second, we needed a theme. Because so many of the folktales featured animals, we narrowed the theme down to troublemaking animals and birds. When Adati Akura, born in Paris of African parents, shouted out, "But birds are animals and can be troublemakers, too!" it was unanimously agreed that our subject should be birds.

Next we came up with a makeshift questionnaire:

1. When and where did you first hear the story?

2. From whom did you first hear it?

3. What qualities does your story have that convince you it is a powerful, entertaining narrative?

These questions were like seeds from which all sorts of reminiscences blossomed, not as an indulgence or distraction but to the express purpose of enhancing the stories themselves, and putting them each in a personal context. These bird stories in turn engendered autobiographical revelations, anecdotes, cultural details of every sort. By the end of the workshop, we had been educated in one another's fortunes, misfortunes, bitterness, and happiness. To say the very least, we learned a lot about one another.

When it came to telling, transcribing, and refining the folktales, things proceeded in as simple and straightforward a manner as possible when you get a lively group of opinionated, intelligent, moody, humorous, melancholy, and joyful people together in the same room, with different languages flying every which way and everyone eager to tell stories! There was much laughter, much argument, much friendship. Sometimes we fell as quiet as monks in a stone hut; other times pandemonium reigned, a cacophony, and I simply could not fend off the obvious thought that we sounded like a flock of squabbling birds. I recall that one night a custodian opened the classroom door and said with some alarm, "Just what's going on in here?" He was immediately invited in, sat down, and listened to a story called "Why the Emu Can't Fly," from Australia. The custodian, who was from Kenya, attended two more sessions.

As for the storytellers' own experiences, let them speak for themselves.

May Nunaburruro, a woman born of a Dutch mother and aboriginal father, said of her story, "The Disobedient Pelican Daughter": "My father told me this story. He heard it while growing up in the bush. He dreamed it over and over, and told it to me. My little sister would sit there, too. Whenever my father said the word *disobedient*, he'd tap my sister on top of her head and she would laugh. My sister loved thinking of herself as the pelican daughter in this story. Secretly, though, I thought *I* was the pelican daughter."

Before he read "The Troll and the Scarf Made of Crows," Anders Hove, who was raised in a small Norwegian village by the sea, told us: "My father used to sit us down around the table—an old oak table like the one in the story—right after dinner. He'd say, 'Time for trolls!' That's how he always started out. It was to us children an important announcement. After hearing his traditional stories, there was never any doubt in my mind that trolls had always been around, were still around, always would be."

The lovely story "The Beautiful Quail" was brought to the workshop by Keiko Inuoe, daughter of a Japanese father and a Sri Lankan mother. Although born in Japan, she spent most of her childhood and young adulthood in Sri Lanka. She said: "One thing I loved about stories I heard as a child was how secret worlds opened up to us. The world of animals. The thoughts of animals. Everything outside in the forest or the rivers was at once familiar and unfamiliar, and there were all of these forest spirits, too. I would lie awake at night with an old electric fan on the bedside table and listen to birdsong. Birds sang all night. That is not true of everywhere in the world, I know. To be truthful, in the stories of my childhood, when animals were philosophical, it never surprised me. I had soon come to expect it of them."

Adati Adura first heard "The Bird Who Sang Like a Warthog" in his father's village in Matebeleland, Africa, in his father's dialect, which his family spoke at home. He later translated the story into written French. In the workshop he translated it into English. Though he had navigated the story through several languages, Adati Akura said, somewhat wistfully: "My story will always come back to me first in my African language, next perhaps in French, then lastly in English. The mind has to do a lot of work! And it will always be that way with me—thinking in one language, speaking and writing in another!"

Chang Chung-su, who brought "The Swan-Scholar's Great Secret" to the workshop, said: "I remember birds kept in bamboo cages in a marketplace in China when I was little. But birds were a rare thing to see. Many hundreds of thousands of birds disappeared during Mao's time—for food! Birds disappeared all throughout China. I was at once saddened by birds in captivity and happy whenever I saw a wild bird, which was not often. Now, here in Washington, D.C., I go to the National Zoo almost every weekend to look at birds, or drive to the ocean to see wild birds."

Five years after the workshops ended, I received a letter from Adati Akura. He caught me up on family gossip, and on news of his own work and his travels in Europe and Africa as a photographer's assistant for a major newspaper. He also referred to the workshop itself. "I look forward to the book," he wrote, "and hope it might deliver laughter, tears, and wonderful thoughts about the wild birds all around us."

I simply could not put my own hopes for this collection more eloquently.